FOCUS ON THE FAMILY PRESENTS

Doomsday in Pompeii

BOOK 16

**MARIANNE HERING • PAUL MCCUSKER
ILLUSTRATED BY DAVID HOHN**

TYNDALE

FOCUS ON THE FAMILY • ADVENTURES IN ODYSSEY®
TYNDALE HOUSE PUBLISHERS, INC. • CAROL STREAM, ILLINOIS

To Chase

—MKH

Doomsday in Pompeii
© 2015 Focus on the Family

ISBN: 978-1-58997-803-4

A Focus on the Family book published by Tyndale House Publishers, Inc.,
Carol Stream, Illinois 60188.

Focus on the Family and Adventures in Odyssey, and the accompanying
logos and designs, are federally registered trademarks, and The Imagination
Station is a federally registered trademark of Focus on the Family, 8605
Explorer Drive, Colorado Springs, CO 80920.

TYNDALE and Tyndale's quill logo are registered trademarks of Tyndale House
Publishers, Inc.

With the exception of known historical figures, all characters are the product
of the authors' imaginations.

Cover design by Michael Heath | Magnus Creative

Library of Congress Cataloging-in-Publication Data for this title is available at
http://www.loc.gov.

Printed in the United States of America
2 3 4 5 6 7 8 9 /20 19 18 17 16 15

For manufacturing information regarding this product, please
call 1-800-323-9400.

Contents

Eugene

Gray clouds covered the Odyssey sky. The misty morning drizzle had turned to rain.

Patrick stopped on the sidewalk. He pulled up the hood on his sweatshirt.

Patrick was on his way to the public library to meet Beth. But the rain changed his mind. Whit's End was closer. And more fun.

Patrick took a quick right and jogged to the front door. Suddenly the sky flashed orange and white with lightning.

Patrick silently counted, One Mississippi. Two Mississippi . . .

Boom! The thunder came.

The lightning was less than a mile away.

Patrick pushed open the door. He heard the bell above the door jingle. He also heard a familiar voice.

"Greetings," said Eugene Meltsner. Eugene often worked at the ice-cream counter at Whit's End. Today he was fixing a large blender.

There were no other guests in the ice-cream shop. The storm must have kept people at home. He set his backpack under a table. Then he pushed back his hood.

"Hi, Eugene," Patrick said. "Where is Mr. Whittaker?"

Mr. Whittaker, also called Whit, owned Whit's End. He was an older, mysterious inventor.

"Mr. Whittaker is attending a board meeting for the Universal Press Foundation," Eugene said.

"Does that mean he's not here?" Patrick asked.

"Yes," Eugene said. "Mr. Whittaker is required to attend all strategic gatherings."

Eugene liked to use big words in long sentences.

"So he's not here," Patrick said. He wanted to make sure.

"He is not." Eugene smiled. "May I assist you in Mr. Whittaker's absence?" he asked.

"I don't know," Patrick said. "I need help with a report for school. It's about soccer."

"I know more about sports than some

people suspect," Eugene said. "Or you could use one of our computers to access the Internet as a research tool."

Patrick shook his head. "My teacher, Mrs. McNeill, said we can't use the Internet."

Eugene asked. "So you may use only books?"

"What else is there?" Patrick asked.

Eugene adjusted his large, round glasses. He picked up the blender. "Well, Mr. Whittaker has created a few options," he said. "Come with me."

Eugene led Patrick to the workshop in the basement of Whit's End. That was where Whit tinkered with many of his inventions.

One of those inventions was called the Imagination Station. It was kind of like a time machine.

"Are you familiar with the Imagination

Station?" Eugene asked. He set the blender on a table.

Patrick walked over to the invention. It looked like the front end of a helicopter. "I've been in it a few times," Patrick said, smiling.

"Perhaps we can program the Imagination Station to assist your research about soccer," Eugene said. "What would you like to know?"

"I'm writing about the very first World Cup event," Patrick said.

"Ah yes," Eugene said. "That was in the thirties, I believe. I'll input the program."

"Thanks!" Patrick said. He pushed a button, and the door slid open. He climbed inside the machine.

The dashboard twinkled with different colored lights. He sat in one of the two seats. The empty seat reminded him that his cousin Beth wasn't there. He felt funny about that.

The cousins had been on many exciting adventures in the Imagination Station. They had opened an ancient Egyptian tomb. They had battled a dark knight. They had even caught a spy for George Washington.

Patrick knew Beth wouldn't mind missing a trip like this. She didn't care about soccer.

Patrick peeked out through the open door. Eugene stood at a

nearby workstation. He tapped the keys on a laptop computer. He said, "The first World Cup was in 1930 in the country of . . ."

"Brazil?" Patrick asked, guessing.

"No," Eugene said. "Uru—"

Just then, there was a *boom*. The lights in the workshop flickered. Then they turned bright again.

"That was close," Patrick said. "Are we safe?" He thought about his parents at home. They were probably unplugging all the appliances and technical equipment.

Eugene moved to a wall. He flung open a metal panel. "We have surge protectors for the entire shop," he said. "Several lightning rods have also been installed."

Another *kaboom* rocked Whit's End.

The lights flickered again. This time the room was dark for three or four seconds.

Then the lights came on and stayed on.

"The city could lose power. But we have a large propane tank outside," Eugene said.

"The tank is attached to that generator," Eugene told Patrick. He pointed to a long machine on wheels. "When the electricity goes off, the propane-powered generator kicks in. The emergency power is already hooked up to the workshop. It's as good as using normal electricity."

Patrick was impressed. "You guys have thought of everything," he said.

"We do our best," Eugene said. He returned to the laptop and began typing. "Are you ready for the first World Cup in Uruguay?" he asked.

Patrick leaned back in the seat. "I'm ready! Just don't tell me who wins. I want to be surprised."

Eugene chuckled. He pressed a button. The door sealed shut.

Patrick reached forward and pushed the red button.

The machine started to shake. It rumbled. Then he heard a loud sound as if someone had popped a bike tire.

The lights on the Imagination Station's dashboard flashed wildly. The needles on the meters swung back and forth. *Was that lightning?* he wondered.

Suddenly everything went dark.

The Dog

The doors on each side of the Imagination Station opened.

Patrick was suddenly afraid that the Imagination Station was on fire. He jumped out of the machine. He took a few steps. Then he turned around to make sure everything was all right.

The machine faded and disappeared.

Patrick looked around. The morning sun was low in the sky. In front of him was a Roman villa. It had a tile roof, marble columns, and plaster walls.

He'd been to ancient Rome with Beth. And this looked just like the buildings there.

"This isn't Uruguay," he said softly.

"Arf! Arf!" Barking was coming from somewhere beyond the villa's walls. They must have been at least eight feet high.

A little fountain trickled near him.

He felt confused. How had he wound up in ancient Rome? Hadn't Eugene set the program for Uruguay in 1930?

Patrick wondered if lightning had struck Whit's End. It may have messed up the machine.

The dog kept barking inside the villa.

Patrick took a step toward the villa's front door. He almost tripped over a leather saddlebag. It was the kind a Western cowboy would use. *What's this doing in a Roman town?* he wondered.

Then Patrick noticed the sandals on his feet. He was also wearing a white tunic. A green cloth was draped over his left shoulder. It wrapped around his waist.

"I'm dressed like a Roman. But I have a cowboy's saddlebag," he said.

Patrick knelt to look at the bag. It was branded with a horseshoe design.

He threw open the flap. Inside he found several bandanas and carrots. There was a star-shaped sheriff's badge. And a pair of thin wire glasses. At the very bottom of the bag was a coil of thick rope.

Patrick reached up to scratch his head. His hand brushed something on his head. He pulled it off. It was a brown cowboy hat.

Something was definitely wrong with the Imagination Station.

The dog inside the villa barked again. Patrick now wondered why it was so excited.

Then a voice cried out, "Help! Get this dog away from me!"

Patrick went to the door and pushed it open a little further. "Hello?" he called out.

"Help!" the voice replied.

The door opened to a courtyard.

Patrick crossed a stone patio to a house. The walls held small alcoves. Inside the alcoves were tiny figurines. Patrick knew they were idols of Roman gods.

He followed the barking and shouting. They led him into a room with several marble columns. At one end stood a wide stone table.

A boy was standing on top of it. He looked to be about thirteen years old.

The dog was large with white fur. It barked and growled as it jumped up at the boy.

The boy saw Patrick. "Help me!" he called. "This dog is trying to kill me."

The dog snarled at the boy. It had white, pointed teeth.

"It doesn't have rabies, does it?" Patrick asked.

"No. It just hates me," the boy said.

The dog glanced at Patrick. Then it went back to jumping at the boy.

"Throw something at it," the boy said.

"Then it'll want to attack *me*," Patrick said. Instead, he asked, "What's the dog's name?"

"Umm . . . Snowy," the boy said. "It's a girl."

Patrick crouched down. "Here, Snowy," he called in a gentle voice.

Snowy looked at Patrick for only a second. Then the dog lunged at the table again. "Arf! Arf! Arf!"

Patrick looked around for something that would distract the dog. He remembered his hat. He took it off and waved it. "Here, Snowy," he said. "Here's something fun."

Snowy turned and ran at Patrick. Her paws slipped on the tile floor.

Patrick was afraid the dog might go for him. He stepped aside as Snowy leaped forward.

The dog caught hold of the hat with her teeth.

Patrick let go.

The dog shook the hat back and forth. It looked at Patrick and wagged its tail. Then it

dropped the hat at Patrick's feet.

"She wants you to play," the boy said. "Keep her distracted so I can get down."

Patrick picked up the hat.

The dog jumped at it again.

Soon Patrick had the dog playing a friendly game of tug-of-war.

"Take Snowy outside," the boy said. "There's a collar and chain near the fountain. Chain her up so she can't get loose again."

Patrick grabbed the hat with both hands.

The dog held on to the other end.

Patrick tugged and pulled the dog outside to the fountain.

The chain lay on the ground. A leather collar was attached to one end.

Patrick yanked the hat away from the dog. Then he threw the hat a few feet away. The dog jumped at the hat.

Snowy trotted back to Patrick. She dropped the hat at Patrick's feet.

Patrick quickly fastened the collar around her neck. He then latched the chain to the collar.

Snowy looked at him with sad eyes. The dog seemed to know she had been tricked.

Patrick gave her a pat on the head. "Bye-bye, Snowy," he said.

Snowy licked his hand. Then she lay down and chewed on the hat.

Patrick went back into the villa. The boy was no longer on the table. Patrick heard a noise from another room. He followed the sound deep into the villa.

He came to a bedroom. The boy was kneeling over a large bag. It looked as if it had been dropped. Jewelry and gold candlesticks spilled out of it.

The boy saw Patrick and leaped to his feet. "Ah!" he called out. He was taller and huskier than Patrick had realized.

"What's going on here?" Patrick asked.

Suddenly the boy dropped to his knees in front of Patrick.

"I, Junius, am at your service," he said. Junius quickly grabbed the hem of Patrick's tunic and kissed it.

Patrick jumped back. "Stop that!" he said.

"It's customary for a slave to give thanks this way," Junius said. "You saved me from the dog."

Patrick took a closer look at Junius's tunic. It was plain white, the clothes of a slave.

"Please get up," Patrick said.

Junius obeyed.

"Where is your master?" Patrick asked.

"My master has departed," Junius said.

"He has left me to pack some of his valuables. But there's something he wants that I can't get."

Junius pointed to an alcove in the wall. It had a metal grate in front of it. The grate was held shut by a lock.

Patrick stepped closer. He could see through the bars. Inside were several small gold statues.

"My arm won't fit through the bars," Junius said.

"Mine will fit," Patrick said.

"Please save me from a terrible beating. I need those gold figures for my master," Junius said. "Will you get them for me?"

The job seemed easy enough. Patrick started to reach through the bars. Then he stopped.

"Why didn't your master leave you the

key?" Patrick asked.

Junius looked surprised by the question. He paused for a moment. Then he said, "My master was ill from the air. It gave him a horrible cough. He left quickly without leaving me the key."

Patrick's eye went to a window on the far wall. The air was certainly thick. It looked like car exhaust.

Something didn't seem right to Patrick. But he shrugged it off.

Patrick turned to the alcove. He slipped his arm through the bars. But he saw deep grooves in the plaster around the grate. It looked as if someone had tried to pry it off.

Patrick withdrew his arm.

Junius groaned.

"Why didn't the dog know you?" Patrick asked him. "She would know you if you lived in this house."

Junius moved over to the bag on the floor. He pushed the jewelry and other items back inside. "That dog never liked me," he said. "By the way, what are *you* doing here?"

Patrick wasn't sure how to answer.

"You're not looting, are you?" Junius asked. "Are you a thief?"

"No!" Patrick said. "I was out front and heard the dog barking. Then you started shouting."

Junius picked up the bag. Everything inside banged and jangled. "Are you going to get those gold figures or not?"

Patrick looked at Junius and the bag. He thought about the lock and the grate and the dog. His mouth fell open. "You're stealing these things," he said.

Junius snickered. "It's not stealing if the

owners have abandoned them," he said.

"Abandoned them?" Patrick asked. "Why would the owners do that?"

Junius looked at Patrick as if he had said something stupid.

"The smoke on the mountain," Junius said. He slung the bag over his shoulder.

"What mountain?" Patrick asked.

Junius nodded to the window.

Patrick hurried over and looked outside. He saw a large mountain to the left. A thin column of smoke rose from the top.

His mind raced. Why had the Imagination Station sent him here?

"What's happening on the mountain?" Patrick asked as he turned around.

Junius was gone.

Beth

Beth looked at the clock. *This is just like Patrick*, she thought. He was a half hour late. He should be at the library by now.

She looked out the window. The rain had become a drizzle. She thought, *It's because of the rain. He stayed home.*

Beth put on her raincoat. She made her way outside. The columns of the Odyssey library dripped from the rain. She opened up a yellow polka-dot umbrella and hurried off.

Whit's End, she thought. Patrick would most likely be there.

Beth sidestepped huge puddles. She stayed away from the street. Large fans of water sprayed up from the passing cars.

Beth was half a block away from Whit's End. Just then, a lightning bolt lit up the sky.

Kaboom!

Beth shrieked. The flash was so bright, it hurt her eyes. The noise was loud. It pounded in her ears. The hairs on her arms stood straight up. And the skin on the back of her neck tingled.

That was too close, she thought.

Beth hurried up the steps and inside Whit's End. The ice-cream shop smelled of hot chocolate. She looked around. No one was there.

She took off her raincoat. She hung it on

the coat rack. Then she folded the umbrella and shoved it into a large stand.

Beth went to the counter. "Is anyone here?" she called out. "Mr. Whittaker? Connie? Eugene?"

No one answered.

Beth slipped behind the counter. She pushed through the swinging door that led to the kitchen. It was empty.

She saw an intercom on the wall next to the door. She pushed one of the buttons. "Is anybody here?" she asked. "Mr. Whittaker?"

A few seconds passed. The intercom suddenly buzzed. She heard static. Then came a series of broken words: "In workshop . . . come down . . . lightning . . ."

Beth recognized Eugene's voice. *He must be in the workshop*, she thought.

Beth went to the workshop door and down

the stairs. She looked around the workshop. Many of Mr. Whittaker's inventions were on. Some had lights that blinked like Christmas trees. Others hummed loudly. She smelled a faint musty burning odor.

"Eugene?" she called out.

"Here!" Eugene said. He stood next to the wall near the Imagination Station. He was flipping levers on a large control panel.

Beth looked at the Imagination Station. Patrick's backpack lay next to it.

"Hi, Eugene," Beth said. "What's wrong?"

Eugene turned around. His thick, brown hair was covering his forehead and part of his glasses. He pushed it back and said, "It would seem that a sudden electrical surge of remarkable magnitude has circumvented our protective systems and interfered with—"

"You mean a lightning bolt fried the

circuits?" Beth asked.

"Exactly," Eugene said. "I'm glad you're here. Would you assist me by reading the gauges on the Mega-Mix-O-Matic? I'll attempt to adjust the circuits accordingly."

The Mega-Mix-O-Matic was a large, voice-activated blender created by Mr. Whittaker. It could create dozens of ice-cream sundaes in just minutes. The kids loved to watch it work.

Then one day it began to throw the ice cream, bananas, and syrup at the customers. Whit moved the machine to the workshop for repairs.

Beth walked toward the blender. Then she noticed that the display on the Imagination Station was flashing. She went to the small screen. "Eugene," she said, "is Patrick on an adventure?"

"Indeed," he said.

"But there's an error message on the display," she said.

Eugene came quickly around the machine to look over her shoulder. "An error message?" He went to a laptop and typed. He looked up again. The error signal still flashed.

"No," he said softly.

Eugene knelt behind the Imagination Station. He muttered for a moment. Then he stood up with a long cord. He plugged it into the side of the laptop. His fingers flew over the keyboard.

Beth watched the error message. It kept flashing.

Eugene made a small noise like gulp. He stared at the laptop.

"What's wrong," Beth asked. "Where's Patrick?"

Eugene looked at her. "I don't know," he

said in a worried tone.

"You don't know?" Beth asked.

"He was supposed to be in 1930 Uruguay," Eugene said. He raced to the Imagination Station again. He opened a small compartment beneath the display. His fingers pushed on the small buttons there.

"Well?" Beth asked.

The error message kept blinking.

Eugene waved a hand at the display. "The coordinates aren't showing," he said.

"Then where is he?" Beth asked.

Eugene made a high-pitched sound again. He turned to Beth. His eyes were almost as round and as large as his glasses. He said, "Patrick could be anywhere—at any time."

Pompeii

Patrick felt awful. He had just helped a burglar escape.

He rushed out of the villa.

Snowy was barking. She was also pulling hard on the chain.

Patrick looked for Junius. But the burglar was long gone.

"I'm sorry, Snowy," Patrick said. He stroked the dog's ear. "It's all my fault. You had him trapped. I let him go."

Patrick saw an empty clay dish by the fountain. He filled it up with water. Then he set it down for Snowy.

"I hope your family returns soon," he said.

Snowy picked up the cowboy hat. Her tail was wagging.

"I can't play now," Patrick said. "But you can keep the hat."

Patrick glanced at the leather saddlebag. He wondered again about the cowboy gifts. *That's not for this adventure,* he thought. *It must be a mistake. I'll just leave it here.*

Patrick hurried through the door in the garden wall. All of a sudden, he lost his balance. It was as if the earth tried to shake him off.

Patrick grabbed hold of a nearby tree. The ground made a strange groaning sound.

He gasped. *A tremor.*

Patrick looked at the mountain again. A wisp of smoke was coming from the top.

Patrick let go of the tree. The ground was steady again. He followed a path leading downhill. Soon the path widened to a road.

He walked for a ways. He came to a fork in the road. Down one road he saw a city. He could see the sea beyond the rooftops. He took the road that led to the sea.

Groups of people were ahead of him. Patrick approached an elderly man and woman.

The woman looked as if she had been wrapped in a green bedsheet. Her hair was piled high on her head.

The couple strolled downhill with short, careful steps. Both carried empty baskets.

"Excuse me," Patrick said to them.

The couple slowed their pace. They looked

at Patrick with curiosity.

"There was a rumbling a minute ago," Patrick said. "Was that an earthquake?"

The man laughed. He had a bald head and a large belly. His toga was dull white.

"That was just the ground burping," the man said. "Now, a real earthquake would topple the city. Why, I remember—"

The woman playfully slapped his arm. "Don't you go on about the big one, Rex," she said. "This young fellow wasn't even born."

"Things changed after the last quake," Rex said. "People left and never came back. But Juliana and I stayed. This is our home."

"Why are people leaving?" Patrick asked.

Rex leaned against a shade tree. "The wells, for one thing," he said.

"What about them?" Patrick asked.

"They're all dried up," Juliana said. "And

the fruit trees and grape vines have withered." She held up her empty basket. "This should be harvest season. But the pickings at market are pitiful."

Rex said. "Some people are afraid of the strange smells. And the dying animals."

"Mostly the rich people are afraid," Juliana said. "The ones who own large villas are leaving. They're moving to other towns."

Patrick remembered Junius. The slave said the villa had been "abandoned" by its owners.

"Why don't you leave?" Patrick asked.

"We have no place to go," Juliana said. "We're too old to start over. Like Rex said, Pompeii is our home."

Pompeii?

Suddenly images of plaster statues came to Patrick's mind. He'd seen them in a book.

Patrick looked at the mountain again. *Is the smoke even thicker now?* he wondered. He studied the city below—the high walls and the tile roofs.

The people of Pompeii had first been covered in ash. Then lava from a volcano flooded the city. A scientist made molds of their bodies centuries later.

Yet he couldn't remember the details of what happened. *Beth would remember,* he thought. She was better at history than he was.

Patrick turned and faced Juliana and Rex. "That mountain is going to blow up. You should get out of here," he said.

Juliana giggled. "You're so serious for one so young," she said.

"How can you know what the mountain will do?" Rex asked.

Patrick said, "I can't explain how I know, but I do."

Rex laughed and pushed away from the tree. "You sound like the priests at the festival of Vulcan yesterday," he said. "They predicted fire-rain if our temple offerings weren't good enough."

"They're right about the fire-rain," Patrick said. "But temple offerings have nothing to do with it."

Rex leaned in close toward Patrick. He whispered, "That's what I say. I don't believe in the gods anymore." He patted Patrick on the arm to comfort him. "We're safe."

Patrick felt helpless. He didn't know how to convince them to leave. He wondered who was in charge of the town.

"What about your leaders?" Patrick asked. "What do they say you should do?"

"Our senators can't make up their minds," Rex said.

"Where are they?" asked Patrick.

Rex hooked a thumb at a nearby road. "They're meeting in their chambers at the Forum."

Patrick saw a large, flat rectangular area of the city. It had tall, white buildings all around it.

"Go to the south end of the Forum," Rex said. "You'll find them."

Patrick bowed to the kind couple. "Thank you," he said.

"May the gods speed you on your journey. And keep you safe," Juliana said. It sounded like a formal blessing.

Patrick didn't know how to respond. So he said, "May you live long and prosper." He waved good-bye and ran toward the Forum.

Lost?

"Lost?" Beth asked Eugene. "You lost Patrick?"

Eugene nodded. "Inasmuch as he was in the Imagination Station with my permission. Then, yes, I lost him."

"Can't we just shut off the machine?" Beth asked.

"I'm not sure what would happen," Eugene said. "Patrick is in the middle of the program. To disrupt it could do him harm."

Eugene drummed his fingers on the table.

"Then what can we do?" Beth said.

"Mr. Whittaker knows his inventions better than anyone," Eugene said. He pulled a cell phone out of his pocket. "I'll call him."

Beth looked at the Imagination Station. It seemed dark and forlorn.

Eugene dialed. A few seconds passed. He said, "Greetings, Mr. Whittaker. Eugene Meltsner here. We have a somewhat urgent situation at the shop. Please call me as soon as you can."

Beth's heart slumped. "Mr. Whittaker's voice mail?" she asked.

Eugene groaned. "I have to think through our options," he said.

Boom!

Beth clapped her hands over her ears. Everything went dark. She could hear the rain pounding against the building.

"The backup propane generators will kick in," Eugene said. "Four, three, two, one . . ."

A low hum filled the room. Then the lights came on. The hum grew louder.

"I wish that storm would move on," Beth said.

Then the Mega-Mix-O-Matic gurgled. It spat out some chocolate milk. Other machines went wacky too.

The lights on all Whit's inventions blinked. The machines also buzzed and beeped

Eugene went to the control panel. He flipped several levers. The noises grew louder as the machines went crazy.

"What's going on?" Beth asked.

"The electrical system appears to be shorting out," Eugene said. "I'll have to go upstairs to the Master Control Room. Please stay here in case Patrick comes out of the Imagination Station."

"How will I let you know?" Beth asked.

Eugene pointed to a small speaker in the wall. There were two buttons next to it. "Use that intercom."

Eugene rushed out of the workshop.

Suddenly a strange laughter filled the room. It sounded like a crazy clown.

The hairs on the back of Beth's neck tingled. A chill slithered down her spine. She spun around to look.

A large robotic clown was sitting on one of the tables. Its head nodded to her.

The workshop door banged closed.

Beth had never thought of Mr. Whittaker's workshop as a scary place. But now she thought, *I'm trapped!*

Patrick stood in the center of the Forum. People walked past him. They seemed to be going about their normal business. It was like Pompeii's rush hour. There was no panic or worry.

Patrick studied the tall, beautiful buildings. The red tiles on the roofs glowed in the midmorning sun. The marble columns seemed to stretch to the sky.

Patrick felt as if he were standing on top of a birthday cake. The white columns were like candles.

The walls of some buildings had pictures carved into them. The images looked like Roman gods. Patrick guessed that those buildings were temples. He wondered which building held the senators' chambers.

Patrick headed toward a group of men. They were gathered in front of a temple.

Some men were in togas with purple trim.
Some wore Roman military uniforms.

One of the men was standing on the steps.
He held a staff in one hand. His free arm
was raised.

The man shouted, "Repent! A day of
judgment is coming. Jesus, the Christ, will
return!"

Jesus? Patrick wondered at the man's
words.

Patrick moved closer to the group.

"Keep quiet, Valen," said a red-haired man.
"We don't want to hear about a dead Jewish
prophet. We have enough gods to keep us
happy."

"Or unhappy," another man said with a
smirk.

The red-haired man swept his arm wide.
"Over there is the temple of the great god

Jupiter," he said. "Behind you is Vulcan, god of fire. You should give them honor!"

Patrick looked at the wall behind the crowd. In the marble was carved a giant god with a hammer.

"Did those gods walk among you?" Valen asked the red-haired man. "Which of them died for your sins? Which of them rose from the dead? More than five hundred men saw Jesus alive after He was crucified!"

Valen had a calm but loud voice. Patrick moved through the crowd to see him better. He was older and gray-haired. He leaned on his staff. He looked as if he might lose his balance.

"Where is your Jesus the Christ now?" the red-haired man asked. "Show him to me now or close your mouth. You're breaking the law if you don't honor the Roman gods.

Everyone must give their loyalty to the temple gods. And their money."

A few men in the crowd shouted out, "We are proud to be Romans. Honor to Jupiter and Juno! Hail Senator Rufus!"

"Repent!" Valen said, shouting over the men.

Valen stepped toward the red-haired senator. "The gods of your fathers are made of stone and wood," he said. "They do not live. They cannot hear you or help you. Turn now and worship the living God! Repent or He will judge you, Rufus. Seek His mercy before it's too late."

The senator roared and lunged forward. He shoved the older man in the chest.

Valen stumbled backward but stayed standing.

"Arrest him!" Senator Rufus shouted to

the guards.

A Roman soldier stepped forward. His spear was pointed at Valen. In an instant, Patrick stood in front of Valen.

"Don't hurt him!" Patrick shouted at the senator and the guard. "Haven't you heard of free speech?" he asked.

"How dare you!" Senator Rufus shouted. He face was red with rage. One fist was clenched at his side. His other hand was raised in anger. "Am I to be rebuked by an old man and a boy?"

"But he's telling you the truth!" Patrick said.

Senator Rufus waved a hand at the guards. "Take them both to the arena! Throw these traitors to the lions!"

Patrick and Valen were surrounded by Roman guards. The soldiers' swords were drawn. Their spears were raised.

The Laptop

Beth went to the laughing-clown invention. She yanked its power cord out of the socket. The machine's lights stopped blinking. The clown's cackling slowed to silence.

"Who's got the last laugh now?" Beth asked it.

A laptop computer sat open on a nearby table. Beth walked over and looked at the screen. It was dark. She touched the space bar. The screen lit up.

Documents about World Cup soccer opened. She reached to open a new tab. But then she stopped. She should get Eugene's permission to use the computer.

Beth went to the intercom and pushed the talk button.

"Eugene?" she said into the box. Beth was answered by a burst of static. "May I use the laptop in the workroom?" she asked.

Then she heard Eugene say something. Beth couldn't understand it all. But he ended by saying, "An excellent idea."

"Thanks, Eugene," she said.

Beth returned to the laptop. She pulled up the browser's history. Someone had been researching natural disasters. Beth found web pages saved. There was information on tidal waves, earthquakes, and floods.

There were also a few word-processing

documents on the laptop. One had been created only yesterday. It contained some numbers and a couple of strange words:

40.8167 north

14.4333 east

4,203 feet

cave canem

Beth picked up the laptop. She went to the intercom and pushed the talk button.

"Eugene," she said.

The intercom speaker gave a burst of static. In the noise was Eugene's voice. Then the static stopped. "The vast electrical surge has impacted the system in a variety of ways. This may take a while to fix."

Beth pushed the button again. "I think I found something. It looks like a document Mr. Whittaker created. I think it's the last program for the Imagination Station!"

● ● ●

The soldiers moved into a tight circle. They stood shoulder to shoulder.

Patrick's breath came in short gasps. The thick air burned his lungs. He couldn't see through the ring of spears. There wasn't a gap large enough to squeeze through. He was trapped.

Valen seemed to stand taller in the face of danger. He tilted his head toward Patrick.

"Have you heard the good news, boy?" Valen whispered.

"Yes, sir," Patrick said quietly. He swallowed to keep his mouth from drying out. "Jesus died to save us from our sins."

"*Anybody* can die, boy," Valen said. "The good news also tells us that Jesus Christ conquered death. He rose from the grave."

"Yes, sir," Patrick said with a nod. He

silently prayed that he wouldn't die now to prove Valen's statement.

"Lower your weapons, guards," a man shouted. He pushed his way through the soldiers. He wore a senator's toga like Rufus.

The soldiers looked confused.

The man stood between the soldiers and Patrick. "This is the Forum. It is for debate and discussion. We will not have bloodshed here."

The soldiers lowered their swords and spears.

Rufus fumed. His face was still as red as his hair. His hands were clenched in fists. "Cosmus, this is none of your business."

Cosmus ignored him and said to the soldiers, "The last tremor damaged the treasury. We need extra guards at the temple of Jupiter."

Most of the guards hurried away across the grass. Only two remained nearby. They stood at attention next to a pillar.

Patrick sighed with relief.

Valen leaned on his staff. He looked weak again.

Rufus stepped up to Cosmus. He said, "Didn't you hear what the old man said? He dishonors our gods."

Cosmus looked at Rufus and spoke calmly. "And you dishonor our law. Valen is a Roman citizen. He can't be punished without a trial."

Rufus's nose twitched. Then he pointed at Patrick. "This boy defied me in front of the guards. He should be whipped," he said.

Whipped! Patrick took a step backward. He glanced at the two guards. He wondered if he could outrun them.

"The boy was defending a Roman citizen," Cosmus said. "He showed great courage. You will not have him whipped."

Rufus opened his mouth as if he might say something. Then he turned to Valen and shook a finger at him. "Stay out of the Forum, old man," he said.

Rufus turned on his heel and marched away. The two Roman guards followed him.

Valen smiled at Cosmus. "I owe you thanks," Valen said. "Because of you, I will live to preach another day."

Cosmus shook his head as if in wonder. "I saved your life this time, Valen," Cosmus said. "I may not be around next time."

"Maybe next time you will join me. We can preach the good news together," Valen said.

Cosmus frowned. "My wife believes in your God. But that doesn't mean I ever will."

Valen smiled. "One day . . ."

"I'm a Roman senator," Cosmus said. "My belief is in the power of the state. And my duties are to its needs. Which is why I must see to the temple treasury."

"Give your wife, Grata, my regards and blessing," Valen said.

Cosmus stepped close to Valen and said, "Rufus hates Christians. Stay out of his way, or you will suffer."

"If I suffer for Christ, then I suffer gladly," Valen said.

Cosmus snorted. Then he eyed Patrick. "What's your name, boy?" the senator asked.

"Patrick," he said.

"That is a variation of *Patricius*. Are you the son of a nobleman?" Cosmus asked.

"My father is a noble man," Patrick said.

"Well, *Patrick*, see to it that Valen is taken

somewhere safe," Cosmus said. He pulled a coin out of his tunic. He tossed it to Patrick.

Patrick wasn't fast enough to catch it. The coin landed in the grass.

Cosmus turned to walk away. Patrick realized this might be his only chance. He had to warn Cosmus about the volcano.

"Sir," Patrick called out, "that mountain is going to explode."

Cosmus turned around again. "What did you say?"

Patrick pointed at the mountain peak. It loomed over the Forum from the west. "Everyone in Pompeii will die if they don't leave. You can order them to go!"

Cosmus laughed. "You and the old man are a funny pair," he said. "Valen believes that everyone can live forever. Yet you believe we are all going to die."

The senator turned and walked away.

"Wait!" Patrick said. He was about to chase after the senator. But Valen gripped Patrick's arm tightly.

"You're right about the mountain," Valen said in a low voice. He let go of Patrick's arm. "A trial by fire is coming for Pompeii."

"We have to do something to warn the people," Patrick said.

Valen's eyes seemed to glow with purpose. "Follow me," the old man said.

The Soap Shop

"Interesting," Eugene said. "What is Mr. Whittaker's program about?"

"Disasters," Beth said. "But I don't know which one. There are numbers."

More static, and then Eugene said, "Tell me the numbers."

Beth read the first two numbers. "North 40.8167 and east 14.4333."

"They are coordinates," Eugene said.

There was more static. Beth heard only

fragments of what he said next. ". . . an atlas . . . a location in Italy . . . the coast."

"Okay," Beth said. "The next number on the list is 4,203 feet. And the words *cave canem*. Is it the name of a cave?"

"It's not about a cave. It's Latin," Eugene said. His voice was clear now. "It translates literally as 'Beware of dog.' "

Beth shook her head and pushed the button. "It has to mean more than that," she said. "Would Mr. Whittaker create a program about scary Italian dogs?"

Eugene said, "I can't always know what Mr. Whittaker is creating or why. Did Mr. Whittaker *name* the file?"

Beth looked back at the laptop. "The file is called 'Adventure A-D-7-9.' "

"*What?*" Eugene cried. His voice sounded distorted through the intercom speaker.

"What's wrong?" Beth asked. "What does it mean?"

The intercom crackled. Then Eugene said, "The 4,203 feet is the height of Mount Vesuvius. In AD 79, lava destroyed the city of Pompeii. And everyone in it!"

Patrick followed Valen through the city. The streets were filled with wealthy-looking people, slaves, and children. There were stray dogs and even a herd of sheep. Patrick and Valen pushed their way through the crowd. They said "Excuse me" and "Pardon me" a lot.

The smell of roasting meat seasoned the air. Restaurants lined an entire block. Bright-colored pictures were painted on their walls. There were pictures of animals and men fighting in battles.

Valen and Patrick passed by a vendor selling vegetables and fruit. The foods were displayed in baskets. The carrots were as thin as pencils. The berries were pale and small.

Patrick remembered Juliana's comment about the food being scarce. She was right. The pickings were pitiful.

Suddenly Patrick saw a familiar face a few yards away. Junius!

The slave was at the blacksmith's forge. He was handing money to the blacksmith. The blacksmith handed Junius a knife.

Junius looked toward Patrick.

Patrick's and Junius's eyes locked.

The slave smiled slowly. He lifted the knife and pointed it at Patrick. Then he turned and raced away.

Patrick tried to chase him. But a herd of

goats walked across the road. The animals bleated *maa-maa* and huddled together.

Patrick couldn't pass through them. He watched as Junius fled into the crowd.

Patrick sighed. What was Junius going to do with the knife? *Nothing good,* Patrick thought.

He returned to Valen. The old man had stopped at a door.

"This is the soap factory," Valen said.

Valen pointed to a mark near the top of the door. Some simple lines had been drawn to look like a fish. Valen tapped the fish outline with his staff. "A fish sign means there are believers inside," Valen said.

Patrick had seen the symbol on bumper stickers and T-shirts back home.

Valen winked at Patrick. "The fish outline is drawn with soap. That's our special sign,"

he said. "Come meet some of those 'fish.' "

Valen entered the soap-maker's shop.

Patrick followed him inside. Wood barrels were stacked on one side of the room. One of them was open. Patrick could see the barrel was full of ashes. *That's why it smells like a campfire,* Patrick thought.

Brick ovens lined a wall. They looked like tiny fireplaces. Metal ladles and large iron pots hung on racks above the ovens.

The ovens each had a metal plate on top. The round plates were small stove burners. Pots sat on the hot plates. Thick, white mush bubbled inside the pots and made glopping noises.

At the end of the room was a large marble-topped table. Wood molds were filled with the white soap. Patrick assumed they were cooling into their brick shapes.

A tall, thin man rushed forward from a
back room. He had a beak-like nose. He was
wearing a plain tunic. "Valen!" he called out.
He kissed Valen on each cheek.

Valen said, "Grace be to you, Nonus."

The man named Nonus smiled at Patrick.
Then he turned to Valen. "Who is this?" he
asked.

Valen put a hand on Patrick's head. "This
brave, young man is Patrick," he said. "He
has important news for the church."

"What news?" Nonus asked.

"Pompeii is going to be destroyed by the
volcano," Patrick said.

Nonus's eyes widened as large as
quarters. "Our brothers and sisters need to
hear this."

Explosion

Beth hit the talk button on the intercom. "What can we do?" she asked Eugene. "We need to get Patrick back before the volcano erupts!"

There was only a bit of static for an answer. She tapped the intercom button twice. "Eugene! Eugene!" Beth cried. "What's your plan?"

"We must procure supplies," Eugene said. But his voice wasn't coming through the workshop intercom.

Beth turned toward the doorway.

"I'm attempting to find new circuit boards," Eugene said as he walked down the stairs into the workshop. "The Master Control unit in the Imagination Station had a meltdown, to use the popular expression."

"What does that mean?" Beth asked.

"Rebuilding it will take a long time," Eugene said.

"Patrick needs out now," Beth said.

"I understand the urgency," Eugene said. "But I'm at a loss for any other options. The sooner we find the circuit board, the sooner we can rescue Patrick."

Beth groaned. "I'll help you look," she said.

Beth crawled under tables and searched through boxes. She found broken alarm clocks. Copper wire and plastic wire and metal wire were in a tangled mess. One plastic bin contained three-dozen VHS tapes. They had been painted hot pink.

"I don't see it," Beth said to Eugene. "Have you found anything?"

"A working model of the first Ferris wheel," Eugene said. "It's constructed from a bicycle wheel and stale marshmallows."

"How is that useful?" Beth asked.

"The possibilities for harnessing centrifugal force are intriguing," Eugene said. "This could become a renewable source of power."

"You mean to power the Imagination Station?" Beth asked.

"Possibly," Eugene said. Then he frowned. "But there isn't enough time to test the theory."

"Where would Mr. Whittaker keep circuit

boards?" Beth asked. She was trying not to panic.

"The storage room in the back," Eugene said.

Eugene went to a door in the far corner of the workshop. He pulled a key ring from his pocket. He unlocked the door and then pushed it open.

He stepped inside first. He found a light switch and flipped it on. Beth followed him in.

Inside, there were several large objects covered in tarps.

"What are those?" Beth asked.

"Old inventions," Eugene said.

"What kind of inventions?" Beth asked. "Will they have circuit boards you can use?"

"That is a very good question," Eugene said. He yanked a tarp off the closest object.

Beth looked at the invention and gasped.

"Now that's a surprise," Eugene said.

Nonus took Patrick and Valen to the back of the factory.

A group of adults was inside a small room. They were on their knees with their heads bowed. Others held hands. One man led the group in prayer.

"Brothers and sisters," Nonus said.

Everyone looked up.

"This young man has a word for us about the volcano," Valen said.

The church members sat back on the ground. Valen nudged Patrick to the front of the room.

"Tell them what will happen," Valen whispered.

Patrick swallowed hard. He tried to

remember what he'd learned about volcanoes at school.

Everyone watched him in silence.

"Well," Patrick said, "first, ashes will fall from the sky. Then lava will pour out like a river and cover everything."

Some of his listeners put their hands to their mouths. Others frowned. A couple of them closed their eyes. Then they lifted their hands in silent prayer.

"Oh, and there will be poisonous gas. That will make breathing really hard," Patrick added. "It could suffocate us."

Valen put a hand on Patrick's shoulder. "Thank you, my boy," he said.

Nonus stepped forward. "We must leave," he said.

"How?" one of the believers asked.

"I know a captain who has a boat," Nonus

said. "It was still in port this morning. He was waiting for a crate of my soap. Perhaps he will take us across the sea."

One woman clutched her hands against her chest. "There are thousands of people in Pompeii," she said. "They aren't believers! They will die in their sins!"

Valen lifted his hand. "We'll warn as many people as we can," he said.

"How will we tell so many?" asked the woman. "You shout in the streets, but no one listens to you."

"We'll go door to door and house to house," Valen said.

"People may care about their eternal souls if the volcano erupts," Nonus said.

One of the men looked a lot like Nonus. He was tall and thin. He had a large nose too. Patrick knew they must be brothers.

"If we're going door to door, we won't be on the boat," Nonus's brother said. "We could lose our lives."

Valen nodded. "You're right, Octo. Each person much decide what to do. If you want to go to the boat, then do so now. If you want to warn others, then let us be quick about it."

"Where will the boat take us?" another man asked.

"To Rome," Valen said. "The church leaders there will help us find new homes."

Nonus said, "I'll pay the captain of the boat. But he'll want to leave when the tide goes out. We have until midday."

Noon, thought Patrick. *How much time does that give them?*

Valen raised his arms and gave a brief prayer of dismissal. Then everyone began to hurry out.

Nonus hugged Valen. "You've been like a father to me," he said. "Be careful. Come to the boat as soon as you can."

Valen kissed Nonus's cheek. "Godspeed," he said.

Then Nonus left. Valen and Patrick went to the soap-making room.

The man named Octo was busy putting out the oven fires. "This is the end of our soap-making business," he said.

Valen opened the door.

KABOOM!

The earth suddenly shook.

Valen stumbled out the door. His staff went flying.

Patrick tried to grab the doorframe. But the ground shifted too much. It was as if the earth had turned into a wave. Everything rolled with it.

Patrick fell too.

Patrick could see Valen sprawled on the street. The old man's lips were moving. He was talking, but Patrick couldn't hear his words. The explosion had made his ears ring.

Patrick lifted himself onto his elbows. He half crawled out to the street. He reached for Valen's staff. Then his eyes went to the mountain.

Gray-and-white smoke rose from the mountaintop. It grew into a giant mushroom shape.

Patrick looked around for the Imagination Station. *It has to be here,* he thought. *This has to be the end of the adventure.*

The Old Car

"An old-fashioned car?" Beth asked.

"It may have been a car at one time," Eugene said.

It sure looks like a car, Beth thought.

The frame of Mr. Whittaker's invention was an antique car. But instead of four wheels, this one had three. Two were in the back, and one was in the front. The wheels were lying on their sides. They made a platform for the car.

Long metal tubes ran along the sides of the car. They looked like bugles, only a lot longer. The engine block had three small antennas with coils on top. Another large, coiled antenna jutted out from the back.

"So what is it?" Beth asked.

"One of the original models for the Imagination Station," Eugene said.

Eugene walked over to the machine. He reached down to a crank that stuck out of the front. He turned it quickly. The gears inside made a grinding noise.

"You have to wind it up?" asked Beth.

Eugene continued to turn the crank. "Yes. It's self-powering," he said. "No need for outside electricity or generators."

Beth was interested but confused. Why was the invention hidden away under a tarp? "Does it work?" she asked.

"I believe so," Eugene said. "Though I didn't know it was still here."

"Why is it in a closet?" Beth asked. "Why doesn't Mr. Whittaker let us use it?"

Eugene eyed her for a moment. It seemed he was deciding what to say. "This invention was unstable," he said.

"You mean it kept falling over?" Beth asked.

Eugene smiled. "No. The internal power source provided too much power at times. Other times, it made too little. That caused the program to behave strangely," he said.

"Is it safe?" Beth asked.

"It's safe enough physically," he said. "However, the user might become confused."

"Confused?" she asked.

"Nothing to be concerned about," Eugene said quickly. He began to breathe heavily.

Winding the crank was making him tired.

Beth watched him. "How long do you have to wind it up?" she asked.

"Until it won't wind anymore," he said. Then he suddenly stopped. "There. It's done."

"Now what?" Beth asked. "Do we use those antennas to radio someone?"

"Those coils aren't radio antennas," Eugene said.

"What are they for?" Beth asked.

"The Imagination Station used them to track satellites," Eugene said.

"Track satellites?" Beth asked in surprise. "You mean this machine talked to satellites in space?"

Eugene nodded. "However," he said, "that is as much as I'm allowed to say. Mr. Whittaker may tell you more if he chooses."

"Why?" Beth asked.

"Because this invention was a top-secret project for the government," Eugene said.

"What?" Beth cried out.

"I'm surprised Mr. Whittaker hasn't destroyed it," Eugene said.

Eugene moved to the back of the machine and began to push

it. "Help me move this," he said. "We need to position it next to the newer Imagination Station. It has small wheels underneath the base."

The invention moved easily when they pushed together.

They reached the other machine, and Eugene waved a hand. "Get in, please," he said.

Beth was happy to do that.

She sat down on the driver's side. The cushion was lumpy. The steering wheel was small and plain. The dashboard had only a few nobs.

Eugene picked up a large cable. He attached one end of it to the engine block. Then he moved to the newer Imagination Station. He picked up the other end of the cable. He connected the cable to a panel in the back.

She put her hands on the steering wheel. "Am I going to drive through time?" she asked as a joke.

Eugene looked at her seriously. "You won't," he said. "But *I* will."

Patrick stood up first. His ears were still ringing.

The sky was already thickening with gray-and-brown smoke. Specks of gray ash covered his toga. He dusted off the ash. He coughed. His chest ached. He wondered if they might run out of clean air.

Valen sat up and rubbed his head.

Patrick picked up Valen's staff. Then he helped the old man stand up.

"Thank you," Valen said.

The annoying ringing in Patrick's ears had

faded away.

Suddenly Octo burst through the soap-factory door. His face was as pale as a bar of his soap. "We must hurry!" Octo shouted at them.

Then he ran down the street and shouted again and again, "The end is here! To the sea! To the sea!"

"We should follow him," Patrick said. He hooked his elbow with Valen's.

Valen shook his head. "No," he said. "I must tell Grata and Cosmus about the boat."

"But the ash is falling," Patrick said. "The lava will come soon."

"All the more reason to help them. Their villa is on the way to the sea," Valen said. He pointed with his staff. "That way. Let's not waste time."

The people of Pompeii were running around Patrick and Valen. The children, the mothers, and the fathers rushed out of their homes and workplaces. Every face looked panicked.

Patrick heard shouts, names being cried out, and screams. Mothers called for their children. Men urged their wives to hurry. Masters shouted orders at their slaves.

The brick roads echoed the sounds of sandals slapping down. The hooves of sheep and goats stampeded over the ground. The wooden wheels of carts clattered.

Sheep and goats bleated loudly. They sounded like human babies crying to be fed. Birds chirped and squawked in the sky and the trees.

Patrick and Valen locked elbows to keep from being pulled apart. Patrick was amazed at Valen's strength and speed.

The old preacher used his staff to push through the crowd.

"Here is Cosmus's villa," Valen said.

Patrick looked up. A vast, beautiful lawn spread out in front of him. Several white statues and birdbaths decorated the lawn. Flowery vines clung to walls and benches. Three fountains sprayed water more than ten feet high.

A huge house sat beyond the lawn. It had tall, white walls and pillars.

"That's a villa?" Patrick asked in amazement.

Valen pulled Patrick along the path to the house.

The atrium was empty.

Valen knocked on the front door with his staff. There was no answer.

The old man pushed open the door.

"Grata!" Valen called out. "It is I, Valen."

No one answered.

Valen stepped inside. He called out for Grata.

Still no answer.

Patrick followed him into the house.

A *crash* came from deeper inside. The noise sounded like glass shattering on tile.

Valen and Patrick moved through the kitchen. They entered the eating area. Shards of pottery were spread out on the floor.

Farther on, a young man bent over a large bag. Candlesticks and jewelry spilled out from the mouth of the bag. The young man turned toward them.

Patrick groaned. It was Junius.

The Villa

Beth sat in the car-like Imagination Station and watched Eugene.

Eugene raced around the workshop. First he tinkered with a cable. Next he went to the Master Control Room. Then he came back. Finally he fiddled with the control panels on the two Imagination Stations.

"I'm ready to go," Eugene said. "You may get out of the Imagination Station."

Beth crossed her arms. "*I* should go," she

said. "Patrick is *my* cousin."

"But his adventure is my responsibility," Eugene said. "I can't risk putting you in danger too."

"If *you* go, something bad could happen. I couldn't help," Beth said. "If *I* go, something bad could happen. But you could figure out how to help us."

She clutched the steering wheel. She wanted Eugene to know she wasn't going to get out.

Eugene thought for a moment. Then he sighed and said, "You're right."

"I am?" she asked with surprise.

"Yes," he said. "Regrettably, I must allow you to go."

She smiled and said, "Great! What do I need to know?"

Eugene leaned on the rim of the driver's

door. "Finding Patrick won't be easy in a crowded city," he said. "You must be careful. Stay away from lava. Stay away from dogs. They could be have rabies."

"Got it," she said.

"And remember," Eugene added, "the air is poisonous." He wiped his forehead. "Get out if you start coughing a lot. And get out fast."

Beth nodded. She studied the dashboard. "How does it start?" she asked.

Eugene pointed to a black knob in the center of the dashboard.

She pulled it. The engine began to whir. Then she heard a noise behind her.

"Oh!" Eugene said and stepped away.

A cloth roof lifted from the trunk. It rose up and over her. It rested on the frame of the windshield. There were loud clicks as it locked down.

Beth looked at Eugene through the side window. "I'm covered by a giant umbrella," she said. "Is it supposed to rain?"

Eugene smiled. The machine rumbled and shook.

Beth grabbed hold of the steering wheel.

The car seemed to surge forward into the workshop. But everything she saw through the windshield blurred.

Then the dots broke apart. They sprayed out of the machine like water droplets.

I'm driving through time, Beth thought.

And then suddenly, everything went black.

"You again!" Patrick shouted at Junius.

Junius grabbed the bag and stood up. The candlesticks clanked together. "Funny meeting you here," he said calmly to Patrick.

Then the slave eyed Valen. "I know you,"

Junius said. "You're the crazy old man who keeps preaching about one God."

"Don't talk to him that way," Patrick said. "You're in enough trouble as it is."

"I am?" Junius asked. "And what are you two doing in a senator's home? I'm sure you don't have permission. My master could throw you to the lions."

"We're here to warn Grata and take her to the docks," Patrick said.

"You're too late. She's already there. I'm taking supplies to her," Junius said. He hoisted the bag over his shoulder.

"You're lying!" Patrick cried.

Valen put a firm hand on Patrick's arm. "He *is* a servant of Cosmus and Grata."

Patrick's mouth fell open. "He is? But I saw him looting another villa earlier."

Valen turned to Junius. "Is that so?"

"No," Junius said with a smug look. "I caught *him* looting."

Patrick was stunned by the lie. He could only stammer, "No! That's—"

"It's all right," Valen said quietly to Patrick. Valen leaned toward Junius. "Grata won't need candlesticks and silverware," he said. "Perhaps food and clothing would be more useful."

At first Junius looked confused. It seemed as if he didn't know what to say. Then he smiled and said, "Grata hopes to buy her passage with these costly items."

Patrick glared at Junius. It seemed to make sense. But it was hard to believe he was telling the truth.

Valen said, "She won't have to worry about buying her passage. Our church has a boat. It's waiting at the docks."

"Is Cosmus there?" Junius asked.

"He's at the treasury," Valen replied.

Junius's eyes brightened. "Treasury? Why is he there?"

"The vault split open in the tremor," Valen said. "We must go there to find him."

"He's my master! I'll go too," Junius said.

Valen shook his head. "Go to the docks! Help Grata with the boat. Nonus the soap maker will tell you what to do."

Junius gave a bow to Valen. "As you wish," he said.

"We must hurry," Valen said to Patrick.

Patrick took the lead. The three headed for the front door.

Suddenly, Patrick heard a loud crash behind him.

Then Valen cried out.

Patrick spun around.

Valen was sprawled on the floor among the candlesticks and silverware.

"What happened?" Patrick asked.

"The bag slipped from my fingers," Junius said. "It fell in front of him. He tripped over it."

Valen groaned and struggled to sit up.

Patrick knelt next to him. "Are you all right?" he asked.

Valen reached down and rubbed his ankle. "I'll be okay," he said. "It's not broken."

Patrick glared at Junius. "You did that on purpose!" he said. "Why?"

"There's no time for blame," Valen said sharply. "You must find Cosmus without me."

"I can't leave you here," Patrick said.

"I'll make my way," Valen said. "Go. Now."

Patrick stood up.

"Don't worry," Junius said. "*We'll* find Cosmus together."

Cave Canem

Beth climbed out of the Imagination Station. The motor whirred as she stepped back. The machine disappeared.

Beth looked around. She was in a garden villa. A small fountain bubbled nearby. Mount Vesuvius belched out smoke in the distance. "I'm in the right place," she said.

She coughed. The air was sour and ashy. Her lungs felt as if they were burning.

She put a hand to her chest and touched

soft fabric. She was wearing a green Roman dress and leather sandals.

A dog barked nearby. Beth turned just as a white dog, jaws open, lunged at her.

Beth cried out. She took a step backward. She raised her arms to shield her face.

The dog leaped on its hind legs. Then it suddenly yelped. It had reached the end of its chain. The dog tumbled back.

Beth sighed in relief. "Are you all right?" she asked.

The dog stood up and wagged its tail.

"*Cave canem*," she said, practicing her Latin for "beware of dog."

Then Beth saw something unusual in the grass. "A cowboy hat and a saddlebag!" she said to the dog. "In first-century Rome?"

The dog chomped on the hat as if to answer. It shook the hat and gave a playful growl.

Beth felt sorry for
the dog. It
was trapped.
The volcano
would surely kill it.

"Easy now," she said. She took a step
closer.

The dog wagged its tail.

She moved close enough to pat its head.

The dog licked her hand.

"Good doggie," Beth whispered. "Please
don't bite me."

Beth took off the dog's collar and chain.
She dropped them in the grass.

Suddenly the dog grabbed the hat in its
mouth. It bolted out of the garden.

"You're welcome," she called after it.

Beth wondered if Patrick was in the

house. She went to the front door. It was slightly ajar. "Patrick," she called.

No one answered.

She called a few more times. But she heard only the sound of her echo. *Patrick must be somewhere else,* she thought. She went back to the fountain. She picked up the saddlebag. *Patrick might need this,* she thought.

Beth left the villa grounds and followed a path downhill. She walked a few hundred yards. Then she came to a fork in the road.

To the left or the right? Which way did Patrick take? she wondered.

Patrick and Junius ran to the Forum.

Patrick slowed when he reached the center of the lawn. Few people remained. He studied the buildings.

"Which one has the treasury?" he asked Junius.

Junius pointed to one of the largest buildings. It had more than a dozen white columns in front. "It's inside and under guard," Junius said.

Patrick took a step toward the temple.

KABOOM!

The ground rolled. Patrick felt as if he were on a lurching ship. He staggered but managed to stay standing.

Patrick's stomach turned. He felt ill. He leaned against an empty pillar.

Patrick looked toward the mountain. The peak had blown off. Black smoke and fire spouted from its mouth. Rocks the size of baseballs hurled through the air. Melted rock spilled down the mountainsides.

Patrick felt wave after wave of heat.

Junius stood beside Patrick. "Look at that!" he said.

The ground kept shaking. Patrick looked in front of him. The columns on a small temple cracked and collapsed. The roof toppled and fell to the ground.

People screamed and ran.

"We have to find Cosmus," Patrick said.

Junius smiled. His eyes were bright—even joyous.

"Let's go," Junius said. He rushed toward the temple of Jupiter.

How long before the lava spills over the city? Patrick wondered. He also wondered about the Imagination Station. Would it appear in time to rescue him?

Beth headed toward the city. A layer of ash covered the road. She took a step. A small cloud of gray puffed up under her feet.

KABOOM!

The ground jerked sideways. Beth stumbled sideways. She fell.

The ash blew into her face as she hit the ground. She groaned. Her side hurt.

She pushed herself up on her elbows. Her breaths came in wheezy gasps.

Plop!

A hot ball of rock landed a few inches from her hand.

She gasped and rolled away from it.

Another ball of fire hit near her feet.

The sky was raining fire!

The Temple

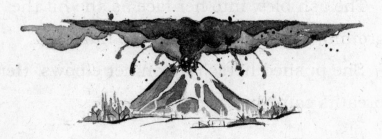

Patrick followed Junius to the temple of Jupiter.

A statue of a Roman god lay in pieces on the steps.

Junius whistled. "Even the great Jupiter has fallen," he said.

Part of the building was also destroyed. Several of its columns lay toppled on the ground like broken pencils. Half of the roof had collapsed. The other half slanted.

Junius and Patrick hurried up the temple steps. They approached the building's edge. Patrick was careful to avoid the unstable roof.

"Senator Cosmus!" Patrick shouted.

Silence.

"Is anyone in there?" Patrick called.

"Help!" a man cried out.

The rain of lava stopped. Beth got up and dusted the ash off of her dress.

Suddenly, the dog ran around a corner. It had the cowboy hat in its mouth.

"Arf!" it barked—and the hat dropped at her feet.

Beth shoved the hat inside of the saddlebag.

"Why did you come back?" Beth asked the dog as she patted its head.

The dog turned and trotted down the road. It looked back at Beth and barked again.

"Okay," Beth said. "I'm coming."

Tail wagging, the dog hurried on ahead.

In the city, the roads were jammed with travelers and livestock. Fallen buildings blocked parts of the road. Beth followed the dog around the debris.

Beth called out for Patrick as she walked.

The dog put its nose to the ground.

Was it tracking something? Beth wondered.

Then it slipped inside a one-story building.

Beth peeked inside the door. It looked like a restaurant. Tables and benches were knocked over. Goblets had dropped to the floor, leaving dark red stains on the stone. Half loaves of bread and sticks of meat lay on metal platters.

The dog crouched underneath a bench. It

bit into a chunk of sausage. Then it came over to her and dropped the meat at her feet.

"Thanks," she said. "I'm not very hungry."

Beth knelt next to the dog and patted its head. She opened the saddlebag and pulled out the contents.

Carrots, a badge, and spectacles aren't helpful now, she thought. But she tied one of the handkerchiefs around her neck. She pulled it up to cover her mouth and nose. It might help to block some of the ash in the air.

She made a loop in the rope. She slipped it around the dog's neck. "I hope you don't mind a leash," she said.

Beth held the cowboy hat up to the dog's nose.

"Find Patrick," she whispered in its ear.

Patrick looked at the roof. "God, please don't let the roof fall," he prayed under his breath.

Patrick entered the temple. Ahead he saw a man in red. Another man in white was with him.

"There!" Patrick said.

Junius suddenly appeared at his side. "It's Cosmus," he said.

The senator and a Roman guard were shifting large rocks. A third man was trapped underneath a fallen beam.

Patrick tugged at Junius' sleeve. "Let's help!"

The boys rushed toward the three men.

Cosmus looked surprised to see them.

"Hurry!" the pinned man shouted.

The two boys put their hands under a beam.

Cosmus said, "Lift on three. One, two,

three . . ."

Patrick used all the strength in his legs, back, and arms. Sweat beads popped out on his forehead. All four of them groaned.

Slowly, the beam rose a few inches.

The trapped man grunted. He twisted his body and rolled away from the pillar.

"I'm free," he gasped.

The men and boys dropped the beam.

Crash!

The building creaked. Patrick saw a crack shoot up the side of a column.

"We have to get out of here," Patrick said.

Cosmus turned toward the standing guard. "Get this soldier to safety," he said.

"And leave the treasury?" the guard asked.

"Yes!" Cosmus said. "But come back after he's cared for."

"I hear and obey, Senator," the guard said,

with a salute. He helped the other soldier out.

Cosmus turned to Junius. "Why are you here? Where is my wife?"

Junius bowed to his master. "My mistress went to the docks, sir," he said. "There's a boat for the Christians. She awaits you there."

Cosmus looked at Patrick. "You're the boy who helped Valen," he said. He pointed a finger at Patrick. "You predicted this! How did you know?"

"This probably isn't the best time to talk," Patrick said.

"You said earlier that all will die," Cosmus said. "Is that true?"

"Not if you listen to Junius and go to the docks," Patrick said. "But you really have to go *now*."

Cosmus looked around sadly. "My service to the city is at an end then," he said. He turned to Junius. "Go to the senate chambers. Warn all who will listen."

"As you wish, master," Junius said.

Cosmus marched away without a backward glance.

Junius grabbed Patrick's arm. "We have work to do!" he said.

Patrick tried to shake him loose. "We found Cosmus," he said. "We have to leave."

"Not yet," Junius said. He pulled a knife from a sheath strapped to his thigh. He pointed it at Patrick. "You're going into the treasury."

The Tree

Patrick glanced up at the slanted roof. "The roof may cave in," Patrick said. "I won't go in."

Junius smiled. "The temple treasury offers more riches than you can imagine. The guard is gone now. But he'll be back. Now is our best chance."

"Not *our* best chance?" Patrick said to him. "It's *yours*. Money won't help a dead person."

"Go that way," Junius said. He jabbed the knife at Patrick. "Don't think about running."

Patrick climbed over rubble and fallen columns. Ash was falling in through the gaps in the roof. The air was growing even thicker. He began to cough.

Patrick came to an area with buckets, bags, and rope. It looked as if someone had been working there. Then he came to a large hole in the floor.

"This is perfect," Junius said.

Patrick peered over the edge of the hole. He gasped.

Below was a large room piled with treasure. It had gold and silver cups, plates, jewels, and coins. The stash reminded Patrick of a dragon's lair.

Suddenly Junius pushed Patrick hard into the hole. Patrick fell. He landed feetfirst onto a pile of coins. Then he did a somersault and landed on his backside.

Junius tossed a cloth bag into the hole. It landed a few feet away from Patrick.

"Fill that up," Junius said. "Hurry."

"Why should I?" Patrick asked. He got to his feet.

"Because I said so. Or you're not getting out of there," Junius said.

Patrick considered his options. There was a large iron door on the far wall. But it didn't have a handle. No windows. No way out. He was trapped and he knew it. He snatched up the bag.

Junius shouted down instructions: "That plate, the one with Jupiter's head on it. The ring with the red gem and the coins. Grab all the coins."

Patrick followed the orders as best he could. "Okay," Patrick said. "The bag is full. What now?"

Junius threw a rope into the hole. "Tie this around the top of the bag," he said. "And I'll lift it out."

Patrick asked, "How will I get out of here?"

"I'll drop the rope back down," Junius said. "I'll pull you up."

Patrick fumed. He didn't believe Junius. But he did as he was told.

Patrick tied the rope around the bag. "Ready," he shouted.

Junius pulled on the rope.

Patrick watched the bag slowly rise. It disappeared through the hole.

Junius's face appeared. "Thanks," he said.

"Throw down the rope!" Patrick shouted.

"Sorry," Junius said. "Thieves are often liars." He retreated from view.

"You can't leave me!" Patrick cried.

Beth followed the dog. It took her to the city's open area. She knew it was a Roman forum. But most of the buildings had fallen.

Suddenly the dog tugged on the rope. It jerked her sideways.

"Arf! Arf!" the dog barked.

Beth went where the dog led. She saw a boy up ahead. *Maybe it's Patrick!* she thought.

"Arf!" the dog barked. Then it growled.

The boy carried a large bag. The dog barked again, and the boy turned. He looked straight at Beth.

Beth's heart sank. It wasn't Patrick.

Suddenly the dog gave a mighty jerk.

The knot in the rope collar slipped free. Beth held the limp rope in her hand.

The dog raced toward the boy. It was barking frantically.

"No!" the boy cried, "Get away from me!"

He ran with the bag. The dog got closer. The boy ran to a nearby tree.

Beth followed the dog. *Why is the dog after that boy?* Beth wondered.

The boy had grabbed a tree limb. He pulled himself up along with the bag.

The dog jumped at the boy. Its front paws slammed against the trunk. The dog kept snapping and barking.

"Get down, Snowy!" the boy shouted. "Get that dog away!" he said.

Beth was about to pull the dog away. But then she heard a familiar voice in the distance.

"Help!" Patrick cried out. "Somebody help me!"

Escape

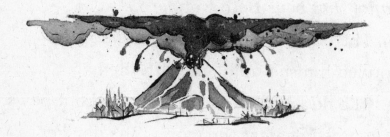

Patrick still couldn't believe he'd heard Beth's voice.

"Help!" he shouted again.

"Where are you?" Beth called out. Her voice was closer.

"Down here!" Patrick yelled. He tried to climb the tallest pile of treasure. But the pile gave way, and he fell.

Beth's face appeared in the opening above him. "What are you doing down there?"

"I was tricked," he said.

Then she saw the treasure around him. "Wow! What is this place?" she asked.

"It's the temple treasury," he replied. "Can you please find a rope?"

Beth disappeared again.

Patrick heard barking.

Snowy peeked over the edge of the hole. She was panting.

"Hey, Snowy," Patrick said.

Beth came back. She dropped one end of a rope to Patrick. "I've tied the other end of the rope to a column," she called down.

Patrick climbed the rope.

Beth gave him a hand at the top and pulled him out.

Snowy pranced around them, barking.

"I'm sure glad to see you," Patrick said.

Beth smiled and suddenly hugged him.

"We didn't know where you were," she said.

Patrick looked around. "Where is Junius?" he asked.

Beth gave Patrick a questioning look. "Is that the boy the dog chased up the tree?" she asked.

"What tree?" Patrick asked.

"Over there," Beth said.

Patrick and Beth hurried to the tree. Snowy followed them.

Junius was gone. Patrick wasn't surprised, but he felt sad. If Junius didn't get on a boat, he would die.

"Who was he?" Beth asked.

"I'll tell you on the way to the docks," Patrick said. "We have to get out of here before the lava reaches us!"

The air was thick. Beth pulled her bandana

over her face. She gave Patrick one to wear, too. It kept slipping down as he told her all about Valen, Junius, and the church.

Then Beth told him about the lightning and the car-like Imagination Station.

Snowy ran ahead of them and barked. The cousins rounded a street corner. The sea came clearly into view. Dozens of boats were moving away from shore. Their white sails dotted the water.

Then she saw the docks and gasped.

Hundreds of people were on the wood platforms. They had bundles on their backs. Some carried baskets. They were pushing and shoving and shouting.

"We have to get into that mess?" she asked.

"Besides the Imagination Station, there's no other way off the island," Patrick said.

"Which boat do we want?" she asked.

"I'm not sure," Patrick said. "Let's get closer."

The cousins reached the edge of the crowd. The sea air was fresher, so they took off their bandanas. They pushed through the crowd. Patrick grabbed Beth's hand and held on.

Snowy barked and growled. People made a pathway for the dog.

"I see Valen's staff!" Patrick said. He picked up his speed. He shouted, "Valen!"

The crowds jostled them. Beth's feet were stepped on. No one said sorry.

Patrick and Beth reached Valen. He was leaning on his staff. Beth thought he looked old, tired, and confused. He didn't seem like the fiery preacher Patrick had described.

"There you are," Valen said. He motioned with his head toward the crowds. "They are without a shepherd. What can we do?"

Beth looked at the panicked crowd. She couldn't think of an answer.

"Where is the slave boy?" Valen asked.

"He ran off with his stolen treasure," Patrick said with a frown.

"Who is this?" Valen asked with a nod toward Beth.

"This is my cousin, Beth," Patrick said.

Beth smiled and said, "Pleased to meet you."

Valen gave her a weary smile. "Do you know the good news, Beth?" he asked.

"Jesus is risen," Beth said.

"He is risen indeed," Valen said in return. He seemed to cheer up.

The volcano rumbled behind them.

"We have to leave," Patrick said.

Valen lifted his staff and led them down the dock. "The boat is the very last one on the right," he said.

⊙ ⊙ ⊙

Patrick recognized the people lining the side of the boat. Most of them were from the church. Cosmus and a lovely woman were with them. Patrick guessed the woman was Grata.

Valen raised his staff at them.

"Valen!" Nonus called out. He turned to a man with a tanned face and white beard. "Captain, you must lower the plank!"

Two sailors lowered the plank. The captain ordered two more men to keep the crowds from boarding.

Valen slowly walked up the ramp.

Patrick was about to tell Beth to get on when Snowy growled. Then there was a shout. Patrick turned.

Junius ran up the edge of the dock carrying his bag of treasure. "Wait for me!"

he shouted.

Snowy snarled. She looked as if she were going to bite Junius.

Patrick pointed to the boat. "Get on!" he said to the dog.

Snowy obeyed.

The captain let the dog pass. "A dog is good luck," he said. "Plus it will catch the rats. But we're out of room. The old man is the last passenger."

The last? Patrick thought. Beth and Patrick looked at each other.

"Please!" Junius shouted.

Cosmus said, "He's a slave, captain. Forget about him."

Junius lifted the bag. "I have treasure! Let me on!"

The captain looked interested.

"What about this boy and girl?" Valen

asked. He was pointing to Patrick and Beth. "We can't leave them."

"Go without us," Patrick said. "We'll find another way."

He looked at Beth. She looked worried. He prayed at least one of the Imagination Stations would come back for them.

Valen turned on the ramp and walked back to the dock. "I'm not going," he said. "I will stay here to help the lost."

Junius passed Valen on the ramp. He nearly knocked the old man over. The slave leaped onto the boat. Snowy growled.

The people on the boat cried out. "We can't leave Valen!"

Valen waved his hand at them. "I am in God's hands! Go!"

The captain ordered the ramp to be lifted. A few moments later, the boat was pushed away from the dock.

The church members shouted to Valen, "We'll pray for you!" and "Godspeed!"

"Remember God's mercy!" Valen shouted.

Patrick and Beth waved.

Junius looked smug. He held up his bag of treasure proudly.

The boat suddenly lurched. Junius stumbled and lost his grip on the bag. It fell into the water with a loud splash.

"Stop!" Junius yelled. He reached over the side of the boat.

Cosmus grabbed him and pulled him back.

The bag sunk quickly.

"My treasure!" Junius cried.

"You have your life!" Valen shouted at him. "Now treasure your soul!"

Beth nudged Patrick. "Look!" she said.

The Lava

Patrick turned to see what Beth saw. "It's the Imagination Station!" he said.

The machine suddenly flickered and disappeared.

"What happened?" Patrick asked, surprised.

Beth gasped. She pointed to the mountain. Lava was now pouring down its side.

Beth and Patrick had to push against the

crowd. People moved out of the way. They seemed puzzled that Patrick and Beth were heading toward danger.

The crowd thinned near the marketplace. Patrick and Beth found themselves on an empty street.

"I don't know which way to go," Patrick said. "Where will the Imagination Station pick us up?"

Beth looked thoughtful. "It dropped off at a house with a fountain," she said. "That's where I saw the dog."

"I know how to get there," Patrick said.

Suddenly the earth groaned.

A crack appeared in the street. It quickly zig-zagged along the earth. The crack split the solid ground in two.

Patrick leaped aside and fell.

Beth jumped in the opposite direction.

The volcano shot rock and ash into the air. A giant fire-rock crashed next to Patrick. He quickly rolled away from it.

He saw a candle shop. "Find cover!" he shouted to Beth. He stood up and ran for the doorway.

Beth cried out. "It's the Imagination Station!"

Patrick spun around.

The Imagination Station stood in the street. Beth raced for it.

Patrick wanted to get inside the machine. But there was a problem.

Beth and the Imagination Station were on the other side of a wide chasm!

"Beth!" Patrick called.

Beth had reached the Imagination Station. She turned around after she heard Patrick.

Beth gasped.

Patrick was on the other side of the crack in the street. It was too wide for him to jump over. And it filled up with lava. She could feel the heat from where she stood.

"I don't know what to do!" Patrick said.

More lava rocks shot down from the sky.

Beth was terrified.

Then the old Imagination Station appeared. At first it was see-through. Then it turned solid.

"Look behind you!" Beth shouted.

Patrick looked over his shoulder. Then he ran to the old car.

"Get behind the wheel!" she yelled.

The door to the white Imagination Station slid open. Beth hesitated.

Patrick was facing her again. "Get in!" he called out. Then he jumped into the

old Imagination Station. He grabbed the steering wheel.

Beth was nervous. They had never traveled in two different machines before.

"I'll meet you at the workshop!" she shouted at Patrick.

But Patrick and the machine were gone.

Beth climbed into the Imagination Station and sat down. The door slid closed.

The old Imagination Station felt like riding in a car. It had wild colors spinning on the windshield. Patrick felt as if the machine slowed to a stop.

Mr. Whittaker's workshop slowly appeared in front of Patrick.

"What a ride!" he said as he climbed out.

Suddenly Eugene was at his side. "Patrick!" he said. "Thank God you're safe!"

"That was close," Patrick said.

"Where is Beth?" Eugene asked.

"She's in the other Imagination Station," Patrick replied.

They raced to the other machine. It sat very still and dark.

"Oh no," Eugene said.

Patrick pushed the button to open the door. Nothing happened.

"What's wrong? Where is Beth?" Patrick asked.

Eugene groaned and said, "I don't know."

To be continued in book 17. Go to TheImaginationStation.com for more information!

Secret Word Puzzle

Find the *Doomsday in Pompeii* words in the letter grid on the next page. (The words are hidden up, down, backward, or forward but *not* diagonally.) Cross out the letters of those words. The leftover letters will spell the name of a man who saw Mount Vesuvius explode in AD 79 and wrote down the details.

Write the leftover letters, in order from top to bottom and left to right, on the spaces below. The answer is the secret word. (We have filled in the first letter for you.)

PLINY THE

Y __ __ __ __ __ __

Secret Word Puzzle

1 lava
2 forum
3 poison
4 slave
5 treasure
6 toga
7 villa
8 Jupiter
9 dog
10 storm
11 Rome
12 rock

```
A S T O R M Y R
V P O K C O R E
A O G D O G O T
L I A L L I V I
U S E M O R N P
F O R U M G E U
R N S L A V E J
T R E A S U R E
```

Go to TheImaginationStation.com.
Find the cover of this book.
Click on "Secret Word."
Type in the answer,
and you'll receive a prize.

THE KEY TO ADVENTURE LIES WITHIN YOUR IMAGINATION.